Personal Best **3**

Thief!

ELIZABETH HUTCHINS

Illustrated by Michelle Ker

A Haights Cross Communications Company

Published by
Sundance Publishing
P.O. Box 1326
234 Taylor Street
Littleton, MA 01460
800-343-8204

First published 2001 as Supa Dazzlers by
Pearson Education Australia Pty Limited
95 Coventry Street
South Melbourne 3205 Australia
Exclusive United States Distribution: Sundance Publishing

ISBN 0-7608-6177-3

Printed in Canada

Contents

Chapter 1

Presents

"Merry Christmas, Mel!" Mom and Rick were handing out the presents that were piled up under the tree. Owen and I had been shaking them every day for a week. I *love* presents!

I ripped open my biggest package. It was a pair of running shoes. Running shoes? I'm a dancer. Oh, well . . .

Next came shorts and sports socks from Tony and Owen. May and Bill had sent me a baseball cap. They also sent some sunscreen and a box of bandages.

Running clothes . . . sunburn . . . blisters?
I was suspicious. I held up my gifts and said,
"There's a pattern here. Is there something I
should know about?"

Mom looked surprised. "You know we're
going to Peakview this spring," she said.

"Peakview!" I was pleased and annoyed all
at once. "You could have *told* me!" I said.

At which point, they all started talking at the
same time.

"We *always* go to the mountains—every
spring," said Owen and Tony together.

"I'm sorry, Mel," said Mom. "I've been
thinking a lot about getting ready for our
new baby. I must have forgotten to tell you
about our spring trip."

"It's something we do every year as a
family," said Rick.

Rick's always talking about families. Mom was my only family until last year.

"Are May and Bill going?" I asked. Rick's parents are cool.

"They haven't missed in 20 years," Rick said.

"OK," I decided. "I'll go."

Something still worried me about those presents. But I didn't want to spoil a good dinner by asking.

Then Owen, on his third serving of dessert, asked if he could be in the big relay this year. Bells started ringing in my brain. Alarm bells, not Christmas bells.

"Hold on a minute," I said. "What relay? Just what *does* everyone do at Peakview in the spring?"

"It's Running Week," Tony and Owen said together.

Rick must have noticed the look on my face. He added firmly, "And all of us take part in the events."

I couldn't believe my ears. "You mean . . . I . . . I . . . you expect *me* to run up mountains?" I exclaimed. "Well, no way! I'm a dancer, not a runner!"

Everyone answered me at once. All I heard was a jumble of words. "Fun runs . . . family relay . . . seven-mile mountain run . . . the Amphibian . . . Invitational Run!"

"Forget it," I said. "I'll come with you. But don't think I'm taking part in a nerdy Running Week!"

Chapter 2

Truce

"Seriously, Tony," I said to my stepbrother while our new video game was loading. "Do *you* enter running events at Peakview?"

"Oh, yeah," he replied, his eyes on the screen. "There are different things to try every day. Not just running. There's tennis and swimming. Some years there's even a little unmelted snow to slide on."

When I thought about it, I realized that Tony had been going to the gym with Rick. And he was doing lots of running lately. In fact, he was looking pretty fit.

As the video game began, Tony added, "It doesn't matter if you're three or eighty-three. Even May and Bill join in lots of the events. You just do your own personal best."

Personal best. That was the way I thought about skiing and my jazz ballet. I decided to lie low and just see what happened. No one in the family said another word about running. For now there was an uneasy truce.

A few months later, we drove up the Alpine Highway. "Hey, it looks a lot different in spring!" I said, peering out the window as we pulled up to Snowdrift Lodge.

"See," said Tony, "you can still pick out the ski trails between the trees. Only now there isn't enough snow left for snowboarding or for skiing."

"But I bet there are some big patches of snow up on top!" said Owen. "Maybe we'll be able to go sliding!"

We spent a few minutes showing Mom around the sky lodge, since she hadn't been there before. As we stood looking out at the mountain, I said, "That trail is the Funnel." Then I glanced sideways at Tony. He stuck out his tongue at me. I guess he won't ever forgive me for beating him in our race.

Then Rick started organizing us. "Don't just stand there, kids. Please carry something upstairs." Then he added, "Let's all meet here in ten minutes, OK?"

"Another boring meeting!" I whispered to Owen.

"Unreal," he agreed. "You know what he's going to remind us about?"

"No, what?"

"The P word," said Owen.

Chapter 3

The
P Word

We all sat looking at Rick. He was enjoying being in charge. He had rules about all of us helping with meals and dishes and so on. "And don't go off anywhere without telling us. OK, kids?"

"No sweat," agreed Tony with a grin. He'd gone off without telling anyone last winter.

I just nodded. If the trip was going to turn into one big sports event, I planned to spend most of the time in my bedroom. I hate being pushed into anything.

"One more thing. So that we have a good week," Rick went on, "what do we all do?"

"Participate!" shouted Owen.

"That's right. You will compete against yourself this week. It doesn't matter how fast or slow you are. The main thing is to join in."

At that, I switched right off. Rick finished by saying that we would all go down to the village to sign up for Running Week—now! But I headed for my bedroom.

"Mel! We're all waiting for you," Mom called five minutes later.

I stuck my head out. "I don't need to sign up. I'll do my own thing, thanks," I called back.

Silly me, to think I'd get away with that! A minute later Rick was knocking on my door. "I want to talk to you, young lady," he said.

Chapter 4

Fun Run

At ten o'clock the next morning, I was lined up on the Village Green for the first fun run. Like the other 300 or so runners, I had my name tag with me.

The tag was the only good thing about the trip so far. It allowed you to get free chairlift rides for the whole week. I had already taken Mom up to the Eagles' Nest for an iced coffee and a chat.

"I know it's hard for you, Mel. But I get upset when you don't get along with Rick," Mom had begun.

"Mom, I want to make up my own mind. You know what happens when I *do* decide to try something. I put all of my energy into it," I replied.

"But will you join in just once? For my sake?" she begged.

So that's why I was wasting a nice morning being part of this foolish crowd.

Barry organizes the run. It was his voice that suddenly boomed out through a megaphone. "OK, runners, five laps around the village. That's three miles. You can walk or run it. And there will be timekeepers at the end. Remember that your time today is the basis for your handicap if you're in the Invitational Run on Thursday."

Rick turned to Tony. "I told Barry how hard you've been training. I think that he's going to ask you to be in the Invitational Run."

"What's the Invitational Run?" I asked.

"It's the only race that has a medal for a prize," Rick said. "Barry invites people of all abilities and ages to be in it. To make things fair, everyone is given a handicap. That means the slower runners get to start first. The faster runners start a minute later, but they catch up quickly. So it's usually a close finish."

When the starting gun sounded, Tony, Rick, and Owen raced off. I walked with Mom. There was no need for me to prove anything.

We kept up quite a brisk pace. Even so, the fastest runners passed us on their second lap before we were halfway around our first. A little later, Tony waved as he ran by with some other kids.

"Come on, Mel! How about a run?" A familiar voice broke into my thoughts. I looked around to find Bill and May jogging toward us. Both looked very energetic.

"We arrived half an hour ago and came right down," May explained.

"Well, don't let me hold you up," said Mom, after we said hello. "You all go on."

So I found myself running along with May, while Bill pulled ahead. As I got into the rhythm of it, I started to loosen up.

"You've got a good running style," May remarked. "You'll do well this week." I didn't tell her that I didn't care about doing well.

It seemed only a few minutes until we could hear Barry. He was over by the duck pond, calling out people's finishing times. Then Rick came running back toward us. "If you hurry, you'll make it in under 55 minutes," he urged.

All of a sudden, I was sprinting beside him and keeping up well. With a final burst of energy, I crossed the finish line in 52 minutes 50 seconds! I was greeted by a sprinkle of clapping.

Now I had a problem! Should I admit that I had enjoyed myself?

Chapter 5

Prizes

All of the name tags went into a box for a drawing after the race—and I won a prize! Well, it was only a running tank top, but it looked really good. On the back was printed *Altitude with Attitude*. Cool!

"What was your time, Tony?" I asked him.

He shrugged and said, "I don't know." I knew that look well by now. He wasn't being honest with me. Well, I could find out later. Bill had guessed that Tony's time would be about 42 minutes, which was pretty good. If so, why wasn't he boasting about it?

Tony went off quickly with a group of his friends. Even Owen seemed to know lots of other kids. Rick was busy introducing Mom to *his* friends. So I walked back to the lodge with May and Bill.

"Next year you'll know plenty of people," said May.

"I don't mind," I told her. It was true. I'd always envied kids who had grandparents, and now I had some. They took me—just me—for a drive after lunch. We stopped at a fancy bakery for dessert. Cheesecake and milk shakes! Yummy!

"Ooh," I groaned. "I'll be bursting out of my leotard after this trip."

"Ah, but you won't believe how much energy you'll use this week," said May. "There are a dozen fun runs to choose from, including the seven-mile mountain run."

"And of course everyone climbs the mountain tomorrow." May looked at me sharply. I didn't answer. So she added, "You'll get a ribbon if you make it to the top."

I chose my words carefully. "I haven't made up my mind whether I'll do any of that," I said. "I only promised Mom I'd try one thing, and I did."

"There's no pressure on anyone," said May. "This is a vacation."

"I'll bet Rick has been telling all of you to participate," laughed Bill. "He forgets that you and Tony are not five year olds."

"The P word. You guessed it!" I agreed. We drove back to Peakview in happy silence.

Chapter 6

Thief!

Rick and Tony were arguing when we walked in. Tony was shouting, "Anyway, it's none of your busin—" When he saw us, he stopped speaking and shot past me up the stairs. His face was flaming red.

May looked worriedly at Rick. Then she quickly announced, "We brought back a big basket of berries to eat after our barbecue. And some real country cream."

Suddenly Owen popped up from behind the couch—my favorite hiding place. He asked Rick, "Well, what *was* his time?"

"Nearly 48 minutes," said Rick. "He says he got tired. He needs to try harder in the Invitational Run."

"Now, Rick, don't forget. We're all here to run for fun," May said.

She was right. Still, something did seem odd about Tony's time. He'd seemed really determined at the start. Yet his time was less than five minutes lower than mine. And I'd walked partway!

I put the puzzle out of my mind for the next few days, along with everything else. Even staying grumpy became a real drag. I found myself joining in almost everything.

We all walked up the mountain and stood at the top.

Tony, Owen, and I took garbage bags and went sliding on the last patches of snow on the mountain.

One night we looked for bats by flashlight, but didn't find any.

Then I went looking for wildflowers with Mom and May. So much to do!

The mountain didn't let us do the seven-mile run, though. That day started with deep rumbles of thunder that were followed by torrents of rain. "I told you it's got a mind of its own," said May.

Suddenly it was Thursday. After a morning of swimming and lazing around, we all lined up to watch the Invitational.

The handicaps were announced. Tony was to start off first with the slowest runners. He jumped up and down eagerly. When his time was called, he shot off like a rocket.

"Go, Tony!" we shouted.

"Oh, no!" we all groaned, when he stumbled on a sharp turn. But somehow he stayed on his feet. He seemed to fly even faster after the setback.

All eyes were on him as he dashed around the Village Green for the third and last time. "He's doing well," I said to May. "No one is catching up to him."

"Good heavens! I don't think anyone is going to," said Bill.

Bill was right. Not even the fastest adults ever got near Tony. He won the race hands down, with no trouble at all!

It was quite a victory for Tony.

We all clapped and cheered as he went forward to get his medal. Then I heard a kid next to me say, "Why did Tony get to start with the slower runners? He's always been one of the fastest runners here."

All of a sudden it made sense to me! Tony did a slow time in the first fun run so that he'd get a big handicap. He'd stolen what wasn't his. Tony was a thief!

Chapter 7

The Amphibian

"That was quite an improvement since Sunday, Tony," I remarked later.

Tony loomed over me. "Listen, if you say a single . . ."

I cut him short. "You're not going to bully me," I said firmly. Stepping past him, I added, "Don't worry, your secret's safe with me."

He avoided me after that.

At dinner, Rick asked, "Is anyone entering the Amphibian tomorrow?" He was happy now that we were all participating.

"I'll pass on that one," laughed Mom, patting her bulging stomach.

"The water in Flat Lake is freezing!" said Owen. May and Bill agreed that they weren't into torture. And Tony stared out into space as if he hadn't heard.

"What's the Amphibian?" I asked. "And why is that the name of the event?"

"Well, as you know, most amphibians live part of their life on land and part in water. So in this event, first there's a swim of about 700 yards. Then there's a run down to the village and back," Bill explained.

May looked at me. "You should do well in the girls' division, Mel. Lots of the good runners can't swim nearly as well as you."

As Tony sat at the table, I noticed the jealous look on his face.

It turned out that May was right. When the swimming got under way, I left most of the 20 other girls far behind. There was only one girl keeping up with me—Barry's daughter, Jackie. But I managed to haul myself out of the water just ahead of her. Now for the run.

With teeth chattering, I stuffed my soggy feet into my running shoes and sat down to tie the laces. But Jackie was already up and running, 15 seconds ahead of me. How had she gotten her shoes on so quickly?

I set off after her, with my family's voices ringing in my ears. Hearing those shouts of "Go, Mel!" was just about as exciting as the finale of the jazz concert. I called up one more burst of energy as we flew down the last slope.

Try as I might, I finished 10 seconds behind Jackie.

"Good job," said Mom. "But I wish we'd bought you better running shoes," she added.

"What do you mean?" I asked.

"Well," she explained, "Jackie had straps on her shoes, not laces. It saved her about 20 seconds. You should have won."

"That doesn't matter," I told her. "It was fun anyway." And I actually meant it.

Chapter 8

Another
Thief

Tony was nowhere in sight when the boys started lining up for their Amphibian. "Where is he?" we all asked each other.

"He probably chickened out because he couldn't wear a wet suit," said Owen.

By six o'clock, Tony still hadn't showed up anywhere—not at the lake, the village, or the lodge. Everyone was either anxious about him . . . or angry with him. Everyone except me. I figured that he'd just had enough of the P word and that he'd be back when he was hungry.

He was. Half an hour later we heard him coming slowly upstairs. He limped in with his left leg scraped from thigh to ankle. His clothes were spotted with blood!

"I guess that monster of a mountain doesn't like me," he said.

"Tony! What happened? You poor thing!" cried Mom.

"Wow! You're sure messed up," Owen said.

Rick checked out Tony's leg. Then he said, "I thought that I told you not to go off alone without telling someone."

"You weren't here to tell," Tony replied. "Anyway, I was bored with running, so I decided to go mountain biking. It was great. But then I fell off in that loose gravel on Old Summit Road. *Ouch!*" he finished as Mom cleaned his leg.

"But why didn't you enter the Amphibian, Tony? It's your favorite event," said May.

Suddenly it all poured out. Tony pointed accusingly at Mom and Rick. "Ever since they got married, it's been nothing but Mel this and Mel that. Now she's good at running, too—the sport I was best at. She's like a thief! She's stealing all of the things I'm good at. I'm so sick of it!" He stomped off to his bedroom.

I was shocked. I had thought that Tony and I were getting along much better now. I couldn't believe that he seemed to hate me.

"What can I do about it?" I asked everyone.

"Nothing, Mel. It's not your fault," they told me.

Mom said that we'd all have to work harder at making Tony feel wanted. She went to find him.

Shaking his head sadly, Rick said, "I just didn't realize. I should have noticed."

He started after Mom and Tony. Then he stopped and frowned. "But what do we do about tomorrow? We really need Tony."

"What do you mean?" I asked.

"The family relay is tomorrow," explained Rick. "It's the highlight of the week for us."

"Let's see," said Bill. "We need a team of five. That's two kids under 15 and one adult male. We also need one adult female and one person who has run the relay before."

Owen counted on his fingers. "The five of us could make a team," he said. "Mel can take Tony's place."

They were all looking at me. "I . . . I'm not sure," I said. "Give me half an hour to think about it."

Chapter 9

^A Toast
to the
Family

I found Tony leaning against the big tree in the backyard. He looked sorry for himself. Taking a deep breath, I stepped forward fearfully.

"Tony, I didn't think about it being hard for you, too—you know, moving in with us."

Tony looked surprised. Then he said, "Well, I guess I could have tried harder to get along with you. I'm sorry."

"Thanks," I said. "Now, about the family relay. I think you should run it, not me. After all, you did win the Invitational."

Tony turned red. He said, "I think you know that I didn't deserve to win. I'm going to go tell Barry what I did. After that, I don't think he'll want me to run in the relay. So will you run for me?"

The next day, our team lined up on the Green. I ran first, followed by May, then Bill. Rick would go next. Then he would go with Owen.

Our first three laps went really well. My time made up for May and Bill being a little slow. Rick ran like a greyhound! Then, just as he was turning for home, a small child wandered onto the track in front of him.

"Rick! Watch it!" We all yelled at him.

Rick jumped past the child. He landed heavily and pulled up, clutching his knee. He limped in and groaned, "I can't run again."

"Quick, Mel!" shouted Tony. "You'll have to go with Owen now."

I grabbed Owen's hand. Together we ran faster than he ever thought possible.

"Come on, Owen, we're going to win!" I urged him. I practically lifted him over the line—just ahead of our nearest rivals. The rest of the family gathered around us, clapping.

"First prize—Snowdrift Lodge," announced Barry. Our reward was two large pizzas. After we got them, we sat on the grass by the river, munching hungrily.

"I'd like to say a few words," Rick announced.

"Oh, no! Not another pep talk," we groaned.

Rick smiled at us and laughed. "No. It's a toast to our family—to the eight of us."

But Owen said, "You're wrong. It's seven."

"You forgot the new baby," said Rick. "Eight."

"To the eight of us!" we cheered.

About the Author

Elizabeth Hutchins

Elizabeth Hutchins is enthusiastic about
swimming and walking, both of which
she does summers with her family and
friends. She enjoys watching athletes
of all ages strive to achieve their
personal best.

About the Illustrator

Michelle Ker

Michelle Ker lives in a big, old, rambling
house with her dog and her cat.
Michelle likes all kinds of drawing,
but she particularly likes drawing
for kids' books.